Dear P...
Your ch... love of reading starts here!

Every child learns to read in a different way and at his or her own speed. Some go back and forth between reading levels and read favour....books again and again. Others read through each level in order.....can help your young reader improve and become more confic......y encouraging his or her own interests and abilities. From books.....r child reads with you to the first books he or she reads alone,.....e are I Can Read Books for every stage of reading:

HARED READING
...sic language, word repetition, and whimsical illustrations.
...al for sharing with your emergent reader

BEGINNING READING
...ort sentences, familiar words, and simple concepts
...r children eager to read on their own

READING WITH HELP
...gaging stories, longer sentences, and language play
...r developing readers

READING ALONE
Complex plots, challenging vocabulary, and high-interest topics
...r the independent reader

ADVANCED READING
...ort paragraphs, chapters, and exciting themes
...r the perfect bridge to chapter books

I Can Read Books have introduced children to the joy of reading since...57. Featuring award-winning authors and illustrators and a fabulo...cast of beloved characters, I Can Read Books set the standa...for beginning readers.

A lifetime of discovery begins with the magical words **"I Can Read!"**

Visit www.icanread.com for information
on enriching your child's reading experience.

First published in the UK by HarperCollins Children's Books in 2008
HarperCollins Children's Books is a division of HarperCollins Publishers Ltd.

1 3 5 7 9 10 8 6 4 2

ISBN-13: 978-0-00-727681-3
ISBN-10: 0-00-727681-8

Printed and bound in China

I Can Read!

READING **3** ALONE

INDIANA JONES

and the

KINGDOM OF
THE CRYSTAL SKULL

MEET INDY

HarperCollins *Children's Books*

Meet Indiana Jones.

He is an archaeology professor

at Marshall College.

Indy's also an adventurer.
He never goes anywhere
without his bullwhip
and fedora.
He never knows when
he might need them.

Indy has been on some
pretty exciting adventures.

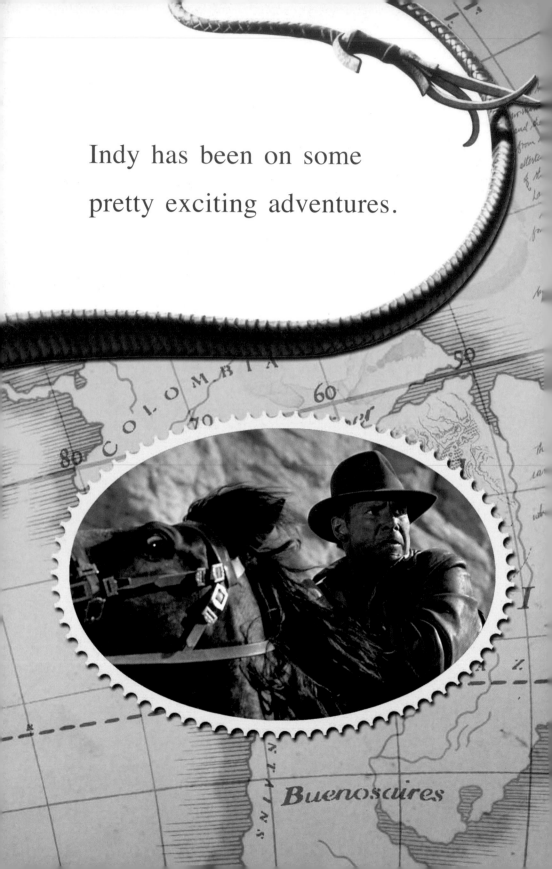

Years ago he found

the Ark of the Covenant.

It is an ancient religious artefact

that had been missing

for thousands of years.

On another adventure,

he was hypnotised

while looking for

three sacred stones.

But he escaped

with the help of some friends.

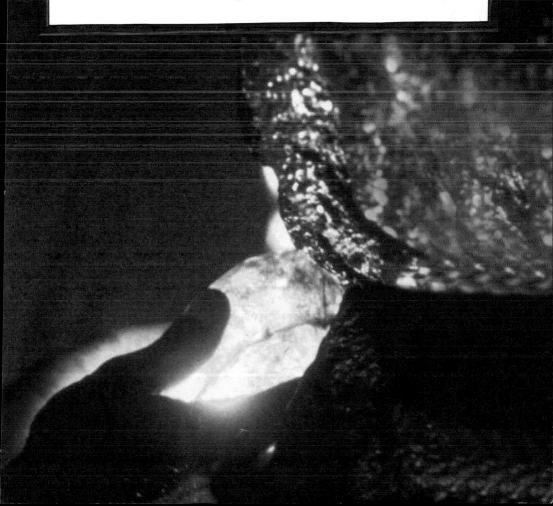

When the war was over
Indy went back to Marshall College
and taught archaeology again.

WATCH Y

Then Indy and his friend, Mac, were kidnapped on a dig in Peru. They were taken to a warehouse, filled with mysterious crates.

The head of the kidnappers
is a beautiful Russian woman.
She is looking for something
in the warehouse and she thinks
Indy knows where it is.

Indy tries to escape but
his friend Mac is a traitor!
He's working with the Russians.
Indy can't believe it.

Indy escapes and goes back
to Marshall College
where he meets Mutt Williams.

Mutt is looking for his mother
and needs Indy's help.

Mutt has a mysterious letter
that is difficult to understand.
The Russians who kidnapped Indy
have kidnapped his old friend,
Ox, and Mutt's mother.

Soon Indy is off on another adventure.
The letter Mutt brought said that
Ox was in Peru, looking for an
ancient crystal skull.

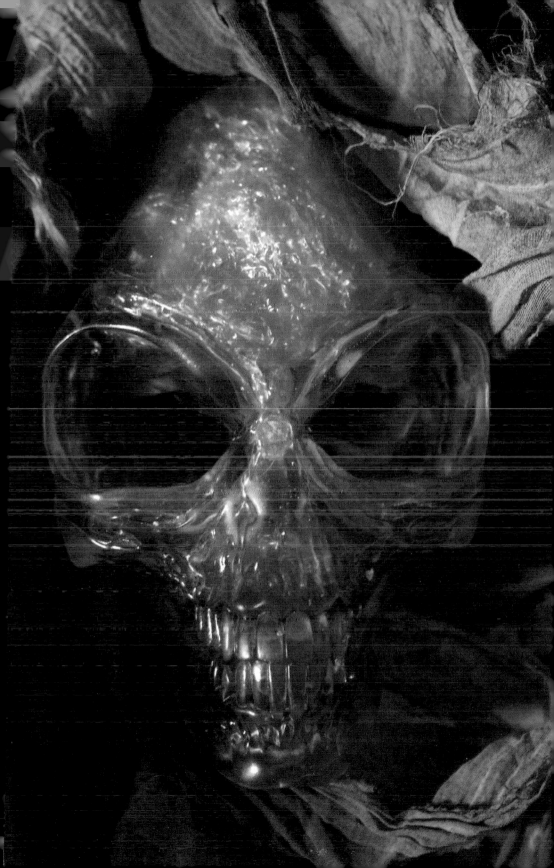

Indy and Mutt are involved
in many adventures.
Bad guys and killer ants.
Scorpions and snakes.
And Indy hates snakes.

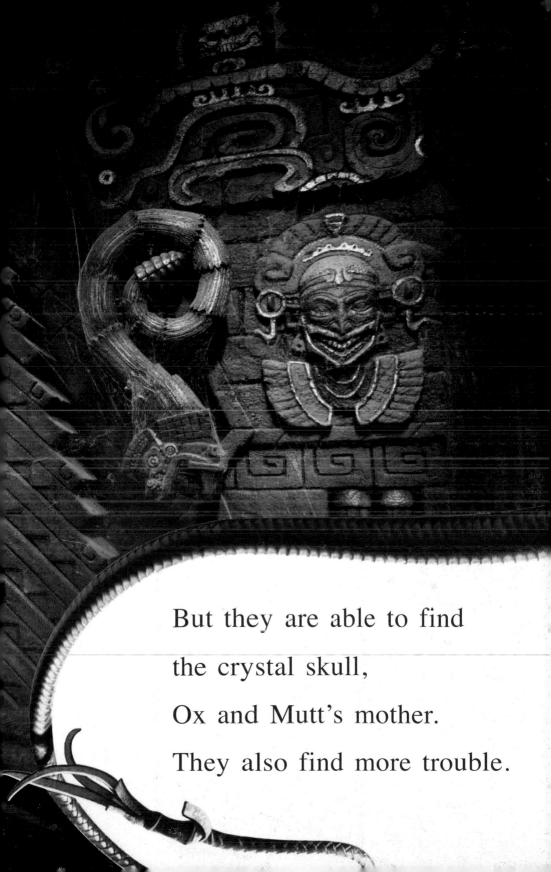

But they are able to find
the crystal skull,
Ox and Mutt's mother.
They also find more trouble.

But that's never stopped Indy before!

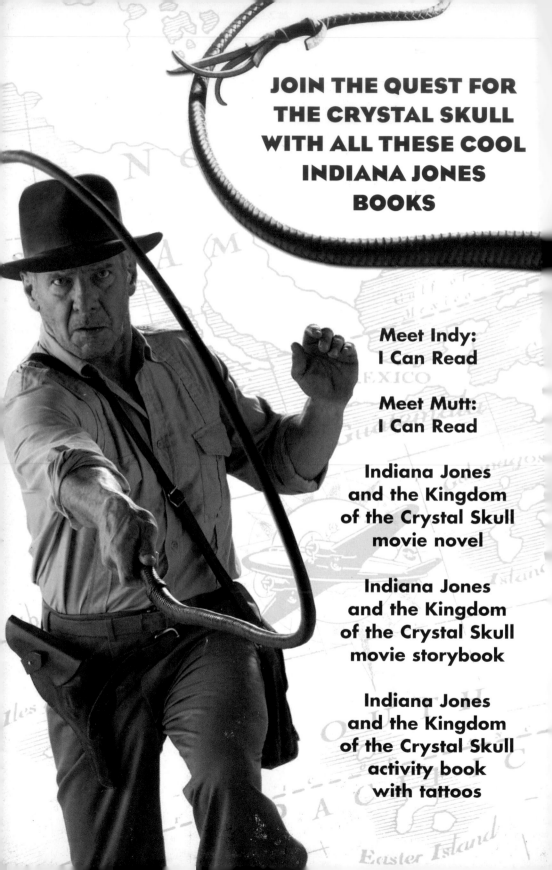

JOIN THE QUEST FOR THE CRYSTAL SKULL WITH ALL THESE COOL INDIANA JONES BOOKS

Meet Indy:
I Can Read

Meet Mutt:
I Can Read

Indiana Jones
and the Kingdom
of the Crystal Skull
movie novel

Indiana Jones
and the Kingdom
of the Crystal Skull
movie storybook

Indiana Jones
and the Kingdom
of the Crystal Skull
activity book
with tattoos